This book belongs to:

....

....

....

Stories
for
6
Year Olds

Written by Nicola Baxter,
Moira Butterfield,
Nick Ellsworth, Marcel Feigel,
Jan and Tony Payne

Illustrated by Mike Phillips
(Elizabeth Roy Literary Agency)

Designed by Blue Sunflower Creative

This is a Parragon book
First published in 2005

Parragon
Queen Street House
4 Queen Street
BATH BA1 1HE, UK

ISBN 1-40544-722-2
Printed in England

Stories
for
6

Year Olds

p

Contents

The Magic Trousers

One morning Billy Watson woke up, washed and got dressed just like he did every morning. Then he had breakfast and got all his things together ready for school.

As he was about to leave the house, his mother rushed over. "Oh, Billy," she said, "I'm glad I've caught you in time. I've got a note for your teacher. Please will you deliver it to her?"

"Sure, Mum," said Billy.

"Here it is," she said, taking it out of her bag and handing it to him. Then, giving Billy a playful tap on the head, she added, "and don't forget to give it to her."

"Why do you always have to say

everything twice?" he asked, feeling slightly annoyed.

Billy put the note in his left trouser pocket. But as he took his hand out, he was surprised to find a £1 coin.

"That's strange," he thought to himself. "I didn't know that was there." But he was pleased. Now he could buy some sweets. Then he left the house and didn't think any more about it.

That afternoon, just before school was over, Billy remembered the note. He walked over to his teacher, Mrs Atkins, reached in his pocket and handed her the note. And to his surprise he found another £1 coin in his pocket.

Billy now felt quite pleased. He had two £1 coins. That was more money than he'd had for a while. But how did the two coins get there? He didn't remember anyone giving him any money. But there was no point in thinking about it now. He would wait until he got home.

After school, he walked straight home. Then he went up to his bedroom. He shut the door, put his hand in his pocket and there it was – another £1 coin.

"That's funny," Billy thought. "Every time I reach in my pocket I seem to find another £1 coin." He sat on his bed and thought about it. Wouldn't it be great if that was true. That really would be something.

He put the three coins on top of each other and placed them on his bedside table. And then, for a laugh, he reached in his pocket one more time.

Sure enough, when he took his hand out, there was another £1 coin, shiny and gleaming, just like the others.

"This is pretty amazing," he thought, as he put the new coin on top of the others.

But he still felt unsure. He had to test the magic a little more. He went over to the door to make sure it was closed. Then he walked to the window and pulled down the blinds. He didn't want anyone to see him. This was a private matter.

Billy reached into his pocket 25 times, and 25 times he came out with a new £1 coin. Now he knew for sure that it was magic, and this magic was for real.

There was no question about it, he was wearing a pair of magic trousers.

"I wonder what I've done to deserve this," he thought. "I really am a lucky boy." But there was just one thing that bothered him – one question he kept asking himself. "How long is the magic going to last? What if it ends tonight?"

Billy wasn't sure whether to stay up all night while his luck was in and take out as much money as he could, or just carry on and hope for the best.

He decided to carry on, but that night he didn't sleep very well. He kept waking up and wondering how much longer the magic would go on. When would it end?

The next morning when Billy woke up, the first thing he did – even before brushing his teeth – was to reach into the magic trouser pocket. And out came a shiny new £1 coin. "Oh, good," he said to himself, and his face broke into one huge smile.

After school, his friend Jimmy came up to him and asked, "Are you coming to the sweet shop with us?"

"You bet," Billy said. "I'll be there."

As soon as the friends reached the sweet shop, they all rushed over to choose what they wanted. Jimmy chose licorice allsorts and midget gems. Andrew went for cola bottles and Rodney stuck to chocolate raisins, which is what he bought every day.

When the time came to pay, Billy said, "I'll get these." He'd heard his dad say that in restaurants and he always thought it sounded cool. The bill came to £3.50 and Billy reached into his pocket and came out with four £1 coins.

His friends were impressed.

"You must be getting more pocket money these days," Rodney said. Billy just smiled. "My granny came to stay and she gave me some extra money," he said.

After a few days had passed and Billy could see that the magic was still working, he felt it was time to tell his parents. But he wasn't quite sure how to go about it. So when his mother said she was going to the supermarket, Billy asked if he could come along too.

"It's kind of you to offer, Billy," she said. "You can help me to carry the groceries back to the car."

But before joining her, Billy went up to his room and took £30 out of his special 'pocket account'. Then he ran down the stairs, but he was running slower than he usually would, because 30 £1 coins are pretty heavy and they were weighing him down.

Mum and Billy spent ages walking up and down every aisle in the entire supermarket. Mum let Billy choose his favourite foods. When they were at the checkout desk, Billy noticed that the bill came to £61.38. His mum started to take out her purse when Billy said, "Gran gave me some money, and I'd like to pay for some of the shopping."

"Don't be silly, Billy," Mum said. "That money is for you. I can take care of the groceries. You should spend it on something you like, or even better something you need." And then she handed over the full amount to the cashier.

A few days later, Billy came home with two dozen roses, which he proudly presented to his mother. She was surprised to say the least. "Why, Billy, these are beautiful," she said. "To what do I owe this honour?"

Billy couldn't think of an answer, so he replied, "The woman at the flower shop asked me if I'd like to clean her windows after school, and I said I would. And she paid me in flowers."

"That's lovely," Mum said, "and to think you did it all for me." She gave Billy a big hug.

The next day Billy bought all his friends more sweets at the sweet shop. He was quickly becoming very popular.

Later that week, Billy's mother took him to the local café for a treat. When the waiter brought the bill, Mum suddenly realized she didn't have enough money to pay. "Oh, no," she said, "I feel so embarrassed. I will have to pay with my credit card."

"That's all right, Mum," Billy said. "I've got it covered," and he reached into his pocket eight times and pulled out eight £1 coins.

"That's funny," said Mum. "Why did you have to reach into your pocket eight times?"

Billy told her about the magic trousers, and when he finished she said: "Why, that's fantastic, Billy! But don't tell too many people or else they'll have you reaching in your pocket night and day."

And how right Mum was. Because it wasn't long before everybody knew about Billy's magic trousers. Things reached a point where Billy couldn't go anywhere without a crowd following him. It was worst at the sweet shop, where even people Billy didn't know were arriving to meet him.

One day, a boy turned up who Billy had never met before. He didn't even go to the same school as Billy. His name was Dan Carruthers, and he was the nephew of a well-known burglar. His uncle sent him to find out if the magic trousers were for real. If they were, he had decided he would have them. He was the type of man who would reach in and out of that pocket until the room was filled from floor to ceiling with £1 coins.

And when Dan saw Billy reaching in and out of his pocket again and again to pay the bill, he knew that the trousers were for real.

Dan rushed back to tell his uncle what he had seen, and a plan was quickly formed.

That night, while Billy was sleeping, a person dressed in black climbed up the drainpipe to his bedroom. Very quietly, the person opened the bedroom window, climbed into the room and crept around until he found what he was looking for – Billy's trousers. He picked them up and replaced them with a pair that looked exactly the same. Then he climbed back out of the window, closed it and slid down the drainpipe. The figure ran to the end of the street and over the bridge until he reached a certain house and rang the bell three times.

The door was quickly opened and a large man stood there with a big smile.

"Well done, Dan," said his uncle Joe, giving his nephew two £10 notes.

The first thing Joe did after letting young Dan out and shutting the door was to hold the trousers up in front of him.

"My little beauty," he said, as if he was speaking to another person, "you have been sent to help me on my road to riches." Joe looked at the trousers for another minute without saying a word and then he added, "How I wish I had another pair like you, but...I mustn't get too greedy. So now it's time to get to work. Why don't we start with a little spending money for tomorrow morning?" And with these words Joe reached into the left-hand pocket.

But nothing came out.

"That's odd," he said, "I'd better try again." And he did, but once again nothing came out.

Joe was beginning to get annoyed. "I

don't like this," he growled. "This time I'll try the right-hand pocket, and something had better come out." But the pocket stayed empty.

Now Joe was getting furious. He grabbed the trousers, threw them on the floor and jumped on top of them again and again. Then, when he was quite out of breath from jumping, he picked up the trousers again, and thrust his hand into each pocket five times.

And five times Joe's hand came out with nothing.

Now he was absolutely seething with anger. "You're not going to get away with this!" he yelled. He seized the trousers with both hands and began to tear them apart. But he wasn't getting very far because the material was rather tough.

"You will not get away with this!" Joe yelled again and, clutching the trousers as tightly as he could in both hands, he ran into the sitting room. Stopping right in front of the huge fireplace, Joe flung the trousers with all of his strength into the flames.

"For this you will burn!" he screamed, his voice now hoarse. And then he stood and watched with his arms folded as the once-magic trousers burned to a crisp.

Meanwhile, Billy was quietly sleeping and had no idea what had been happening. When he woke up the next morning, he dressed as usual. But he no longer felt the same excitement over his magic trousers. It hadn't turned out to be the wonderful adventure he thought it was going to be.

He put his trousers on and automatically reached into his pocket, but this time no gleaming coin came out. "That's funny," he thought, and reached in again. But once again nothing came out. "I'll give it one more try," he thought. But still nothing came out.

Billy didn't get angry and he wasn't upset. He didn't even look surprised, just a little disappointed. It was almost as if he expected it.

"Oh, well," he thought, "easy come, easy go." He never really expected the magic to last.

In some ways he was relieved. Now he would no longer have to pay for everyone's sweets. That's another thing he learned. When you have money, people expect a lot from you. Now he could be his old self again. He started to laugh.

That afternoon after school, the usual

crowd gathered around Billy, but he just smiled and said, "Sorry folks, you'll have to buy your own. The magic show is over." Billy's friends all looked very disappointed and some people walked away. But Billy was happy.

After a couple of days he had forgotten all about the magic trousers. But that Saturday morning when he woke up, he was surprised to find a £5 note under his pillow and a note from his mother: "To Billy, for being such a kind and helpful boy. Love Mum xxx."

Robovac

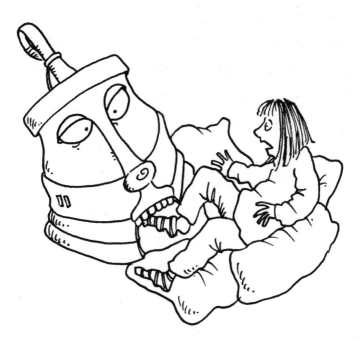

Robovac was bored. Mum had put him in a dark cupboard under the stairs, and he hated it. There was no one in the cupboard he could talk to or, better still, argue with. The only things in there were boxes and buckets and brooms, and a pink feather duster.

"A feather duster!" said Robovac to himself. "What good is a feather duster? You can't argue with a feather duster, especially a pink one."

Robovac was getting fidgety. Yesterday Mum had taken him out of the cupboard and given him some exercise. She had switched him on and let him suck up bits of fluff from the carpet. Then she had pressed a button for the tube to come out of his mouth, so he could reach some itsy-bitsy cobwebs from the top of the curtains.

It just wasn't enough!

Robovac was a super-duper, 'leave everything to me' robot vacuum cleaner, and he wanted a real mess to clear up. He wanted someone to spill a packet of cereal so he could suck it up into his hollow, empty tummy. He wanted the dog to tear up his basket and leave the pieces all over the kitchen floor. He wanted Dad to drop a bag of nails, so he could feel them scratching and scraping as they rattled down his throat.

Robovac wanted some proper work and, if he didn't get it soon, he didn't know what he would do.

One morning, Mum took Robovac upstairs to clean Sophie's bedroom. Sophie was six and not very tidy. She was no good at putting things away.

"Tut, tut," muttered Mum when she saw the muddle in Sophie's room. "I shall have to speak to Sophie." There were clothes on the bed and books, toys and games scattered on the floor. Mum dragged Robovac into the room behind her.

When Robovac saw the mess he cheered up.

"This is more like it," he thought to himself. He could clear this up in a jiffy. If Mum would let him he could suck up the books and toys and clothes in no time at all. But Mum had other ideas. She began tidying up with her hands! She folded the clothes on the bed and put them away in the cupboard. She picked up the books and games and put them on the shelves. She put all the toys in the toybox.

"What's the point of me being here if she's not going to let me do anything?"

grumbled Robovac to himself.

But then Mum switched him on and pointed him at the carpet. With a roar of excitement Robovac sucked up some dust and then tackled a heap of torn paper. Then he put his nose under the bed and sucked and slurped until all the fluff and cobwebs had disappeared. This was more like it. He was beginning to enjoy himself.

He looked round for something else to do.

Mum had moved over to the window to straighten the curtains when Robovac saw Tiny Teddy lying under a chair. Robovac knew that Tiny Teddy was Sophie's favourite toy. She had had him since she was a baby, and every night she took him with her to bed.

Robovac grinned to himself. It was a horrible, scary sort of grin. He pushed the chair to one side and swallowed Tiny Teddy in one big gulp.

Robovac felt much better. He was almost cheerful. He could feel the weight of Tiny Teddy inside his tummy, and it felt very good.

When Sophie came home from school she asked Mum if she could have her tea in the garden.

"Any special reason?" asked Mum.

"I promised Tiny Teddy that we'd have

a picnic today," replied Sophie.

"You mustn't break a promise," said Mum, smiling at her.

Sophie smiled back. Sophie thought she had the nicest mum in the whole world.

"Go and get him," said Mum, "and I'll get the picnic ready. What do you think Tiny Teddy would like to eat?"

"His favourite is tuna sandwiches cut into little triangles with baby tomatoes," said Sophie.

"What would he like to drink?" asked Mum.

"Cold milk," said Sophie, "in his special blue mug."

"Ready in five minutes," said Mum.

Sophie went upstairs to fetch Tiny Teddy. "Where are you?" she called when she didn't see him in his usual place on the pillow.

But ten minutes later, Sophie came

running downstairs. "Mum," she said, "I can't find Tiny Teddy anywhere. Have you seen him?"

Mum hadn't seen him. She and Sophie looked everywhere, but Tiny Teddy seemed to have disappeared. Sophie had the picnic by herself, and at bedtime she went to bed, alone.

She didn't sleep very well that night.

The next day, Mum took Robovac into Alistair's room. Alistair was Sophie's brother, but unlike his sister he was very tidy. His books were in the bookcase, his computer games were on his desk and there was nothing lying around on the floor. The only thing Robovac could find to eat was a pencil wedged between the carpet and the wall. It wasn't enough but, for the moment, it would have to do.

The next day, Robovac made up for it. Mum took him with her to clear up the playroom. On the floor was a brand-new train set. It was Alistair's pride and joy. There were engines and carriages, signals and signalmen. There were guards and drivers and tunnels and stations. Alistair spent hours playing with it.

Robovac was feeling hungry. He had spent the night under the stairs with only some fluff, a broken pencil and Tiny Teddy inside him. His tummy was almost empty. When he saw the train set, he smacked his lips together. "Real food at last," he said to himself.

By the time Mum had put

Robovac back under the stairs, he had eaten three guardsmen, a signal box, two tunnels and an engine. For the first time in his life Robovac was happy. He burped and settled down to a good night's sleep.

But the full feeling didn't last long, and the next morning Robovac was hungry again. As he went round the house, he ate a sock, half the cat's dinner, an old toothbrush and Dad's briefcase. He did it so quickly that nobody noticed. The family was puzzled by the way so many things kept disappearing, but they didn't worry too much. They were sure the missing things would turn up somewhere.

The following week, Sophie didn't go to school because she had a bad cold. Mum made a little nest for her on the sitting-room floor with some big cushions, and Sophie was curled up looking at a book. Mum had used Robovac earlier but had forgotten to put him away. He was standing in a corner of the room, half hidden behind a chair.

It was very peaceful in the room, and very warm. Sophie's eyes were almost closed. She still missed Tiny Teddy when she went to bed, and last night it had taken her a long time to get to sleep.

Robovac watched Sophie carefully. He was hungry. All he had eaten for two days was a couple of fluffy peanuts he had found under the coffee table. He was more than just hungry. He was starving!

Sophie's eyes closed, and the book slipped off her lap. From a long way off she thought she heard a rumbly-grumbly sort of sound. Then it stopped. Sophie's breathing was slow and steady. The room was very quiet. Then she heard the sound again. This time it was much louder. Sophie opened her eyes a crack. As she did,

Robovac roared into life and moved towards her. Sophie was too startled to do anything. Robovac grabbed her book and ate it. Then, with a quick movement, he got hold of the toe of one of her socks and started to pull. He pulled and he sucked and he slurped, until the sock came right off and disappeared down his throat!

Sophie got up. "Mum!" she yelled, running into the kitchen, "Robovac ate my sock!"

Mum looked at her in amazement. "Robovac?" she asked. "Are you sure?"

"Yes," said Sophie, still feeling scared. "Come and see."

When they went back into the sitting-room, Robovac was nowhere to be seen. Mum checked the cupboard under the stairs. The door was shut and Robovac was inside.

"It can't have been Robovac," said

Mum. "Vacuum cleaners can't open doors by themselves. Perhaps you were dreaming?"

"I don't think so," said Sophie, "and look, my sock has gone."

They both looked at Sophie's bare foot. Then they looked for the sock, but they couldn't find it anywhere. It was very mysterious.

More things started to disappear: toys, books, clothes, Mum's favourite necklace and Dad's best tie. And worse was to come. One day Bertie the budgie vanished. Sophie went into the kitchen to feed him and found his cage wide open and feathers scattered everywhere.

Mum tried to comfort Sophie, telling

her that she was sure Bertie would come back soon. However, the very next time she went to use Robovac she found some bright-blue feathers stuck in the corner of the vacuum cleaner's mouth.

Mum decided that she'd had enough. She decided to set a trap.

First, she asked Dad to put a really strong bolt on the cupboard door under the stairs. Then she locked Robovac in.

When she took him out a week later Robovac was so hungry he was almost snarling. He struggled to get away from Mum, and it took all her strength to hold on to him. Robovac knew that if he could get into the children's playroom he could feed on all the toys scattered across the floor. But Mum had other ideas. She pushed him into the sitting-room and shut the door.

In the middle of the sitting-room floor was the fattest, squidgiest cushion Robovac had ever seen. He licked his black plastic lips greedily. If he could eat that, he didn't think he would ever be hungry again.

To his surprise, Mum switched him on and let him go. He lurched towards the cushion and tore into it. It split open at once and feathers spilled out in all directions.

Burying his head deep inside the cushion, Robovac sucked and slurped and gulped. He began to eat the cushion as fast as he could. Feathers started to disappear down his throat like water pouring down a drain.

Mum watched as Robovac ate more and more. His tummy began to get so full it looked as though it would burst. Then, he started to splutter. He bounced around, trying to loosen some tickly feathers that were stuck in his throat. Coughing and choking, Robovac plunged up and down.

Suddenly, there was a huge bang, and a million white feathers filled the sitting-room.

Several minutes later, when the feathers had finally cleared, Mum could see that Robovac had fallen over. He was lying on his back with a large gaping hole in his side.

Slowly Mum went over to take a closer look. Among the feathers she saw Sophie's missing sock! Then, she saw the bits and pieces from Alistair's train set – and Dad's briefcase – and her necklace. They were all undamaged. Robovac must have swallowed them whole.

Next, Mum saw something very familiar. Asleep, curled up in a pile of feathers, was...Sophie's Tiny Teddy!

And that wasn't the end of it. When Mum went to brush away a white feather from Tiny Teddy's head, she noticed one feather that wasn't white! It was...blue! The next minute, a very happy Bertie was sitting on her finger, singing loudly.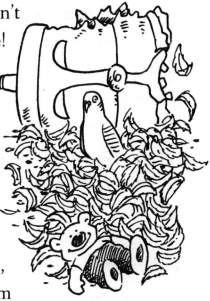

When Sophie and Alistair came home from school, Mum showed them all the missing things.

"Where did you find him?" cried Sophie, hugging Tiny Teddy.

"There's something else," said Mum. "Close your eyes and listen," and she took the cover off the budgie's cage. When Sophie and Alistair heard Bertie's singing, they thought it was the sweetest sound they had ever heard.

It was a very happy time in Sophie and

Alistair's house that day. Mum cooked dinner wearing her favourite necklace. Dad cleaned up his briefcase. Alistair played with his train set, and Sophie spent ages getting Tiny Teddy ready for bed.

The next day, Mum went out to buy a new vacuum cleaner. She looked at quite a few before she made up her mind. This time she wasn't interested in a super-duper, fantastically efficient robot that did all the work for you. This time she chose an ordinary, simple, friendly cleaner that would do exactly what she told it.

Mrs Wolf's Problem

M rs Wolf was a storybook wolf, and she had a problem. She thought about it all day. She dreamed about it all night. The problem was that her son William was not big and he was not bad. And that is the worst thing that could ever happen to a storybook wolf. Storybook wolves are supposed to eat little pigs (always three at a time). They are supposed to gobble up old grandmas (when they're ill in bed). They are supposed to scare little girls, hang around in the dark near flocks of sheep and howl whenever there is a full moon.

But William did none of these things.

At first Mrs Wolf thought that he

would grow out of it. He had been a rather small cub, but his mother thought he would start munching little pigs when he grew bigger. But even when William was fully grown, he only came up to her shoulder. His teeth were sharp and white. But they were not big enough to scare anyone. His eyes were bright and clever. But they did not shine when he saw little old ladies. He didn't drool or lurk. And his howl was quite sweet and not at all scary.

Mrs Wolf didn't know what to do. She loved William, but he had to learn to be a proper storybook wolf. Then she had an idea. She would send him to old Septimus Wolf for lessons in how to be scary. Septimus lived in the Deep Dark Forest. He was a really nasty wolf. He was a wolf that any mother would be proud of. He was so scary that even other wolves kept out of his way.

William didn't really want to go. He had heard some horrible stories about Septimus. But he was a good wolf. He always did what his mother told him. So he went into the Deep Dark Forest for his first lesson in scariness.

William reached the old wolf's lair and took a deep breath. Then he poked his snout inside.

"Hello?" he said, in a very small voice.

Septimus was asleep in front of a roaring fire. William thought the old wolf would leap up and start snarling. He waited, but nothing happened. It was warm and cosy by the fire. After a while, William lay down too. He went to sleep with his head on his paws.

When William woke up it was already getting dark. It was time to go home again. Septimus woke up too. He stretched and yawned.

"You must be young William," he said. "Is it time for your first lesson?"

William shook his head.

"No, it's time I was going home. Would you like me to come back tomorrow?"

"That's a good idea," said Septimus. He was thinking of the payment he was going to get from William's mother. "Little and often is the best way to learn."

That night, Mrs Wolf asked William about his first lesson.

"Did he tell you about pouncing?" she asked. "Did you practise whining and scrabbling? Show me what you did."

William thought hard. He didn't want

to upset his mother. "I don't think I should tell you," he said. He knew that she was expecting him to learn great things from old Septimus.

Mrs Wolf smiled and nodded. "I suppose he has made you promise not to talk about your lessons," she said. "I think I understand. A wolf's secrets are very important. Come and have your supper. I'm sure you've earned it."

For three weeks, William spent every day asleep in front of the fire with Septimus. It meant that he didn't need any sleep at night. So he started to creep out in the dark when he should have been in bed. Sometimes he sniffed around the sheep-pens and henhouses. Mrs Wolf thought this was a very good sign.

"Aah, the lessons are working," she chuckled, rubbing her paws together. "I knew his wolfishness would come out sooner or later."

At the end of the three weeks, the weather grew a bit warmer. When William trotted through the Deep Dark Forest to Septimus's lair, he found that there was no cosy fire waiting. Septimus was wide awake.

"Hello, young William," said the old wolf. "I think winter is over, and I'm feeling a bit peckish. Let's go and find ourselves some breakfast."

Septimus and William crept down the hill towards the meadow. They could see lots of plump new lambs. The shepherd boy was chatting to a friend at the bottom of the hill, and 30 pretty white lambs were nibbling on the green grass.

"How sweet they look," said Septimus, licking his lips and drooling. "Off you go, my boy."

"Go where?" asked William. "I thought

we were going to have breakfast together this morning?"

"Ha, ha, ha! What a joker you are!" chuckled Septimus. "You're going to fetch the breakfast."

"Oh, fine. Where is it?" asked the young wolf. He was feeling quite peckish himself now.

"Over there, of course!" Septimus sounded a bit cross. "The lambs. Look! I think two each will do to start with. You can always go back for more if we're still hungry."

William could not believe his ears. And he always said the first thing that came into his head.

"What? You want me to hurt those sweet little woolly lambs? I can't do that! I always get my breakfast from my mother. We could go and ask her for some."

Septimus suddenly started to look very

scary. The hair on the back of his neck rose up. His lips curled and he showed William his sharp yellow teeth.

"Where do you think your mother gets your breakfast from?" he snarled. "What did you have this morning?"

"Two lamb chops and three eggs," said William. Then he looked at the lambs again. "Ooooh! You don't mean...? She wouldn't...? Not my own dear mother?"

"She would. And she could. And she did!" growled Septimus. "And now I see why she sent you to me. Look, it's simple. All you have to do is sneak up to one of those lambs and grab it round the neck. A quick bite and it's all over. Easy for the lamb.

Even easier for you. Got the idea? Now off you go!"

William tried. He didn't want to let Septimus down. He crept down the hill as well as he could (he was a bit loud). He got very near to a plump little lamb. Then she looked up and saw him.

William froze. Then he remembered what his mother had told him. Not about catching lambs, but about being polite.

"Er...excuse me," he said. "I'm looking for some breakfast."

The lamb was a bit surprised. This looked like a wolf. He smelled like a wolf. But he didn't act like a wolf.

"I'm sorry," she said, "I don't think we've been introduced. My name is Lily Lamb. Who are you?"

"William Wolf!" said William with a big smile. "Pleased to meet you."

But Lily Lamb only heard the word

'wolf'. She only saw William's white little teeth. "Baa!" she cried, and ran away as fast as she could.

"That was not a very good start," sighed Septimus. "How do you feel about chickens?"

"Delicious!" replied William, licking his lips.

"Then follow me, but be careful not to make any noise."

The two wolves trotted over the hill to the henhouse. Septimus looked around, but he couldn't see the farmer.

"There's a nice plump chicken sitting just inside the door," hissed Septimus. "Lift up the latch with your nose, dive in, grab her, stop her squawking and we're off. It's not much of a meal for two, but it will be a good start."

"Right," William nodded. But he still wasn't sure. "Look, do I really have to do this?" he asked. "All that squawking, feathers in the mouth, claws in the nose, all that sort of thing. Just for a tiny bite of breakfast. Is it worth it?"

"Yes," said Septimus.

Then William had a brilliant idea. He looked up at his teacher. "The thing is, I'm new to this sort of thing. I don't know where to put my teeth. I don't know where to put my paws. Will you show me how to do it, just this once?"

Septimus looked down at his paws. He twitched his ears. He gave a little cough.

"I'd…er…love to help," he said, "but I don't really like chicken very much. Maybe we could call in on your mother after all. She might already have lunch on the table."

"Good idea! Follow me!" called William. He was very glad that he didn't have to deal with feathers or feet.

When she saw Septimus and William,

Mrs Wolf gave a big smile.

"Mr Septimus," she cried, "this is an honour indeed. Please come in. What can I get you? A drink? A little snack? Just a bone to nibble on? I hope my boy has been behaving himself."

"I was thinking more of a four-course lunch," said Septimus. "We've been very busy this morning working on howling and lurking. We haven't had a moment to stop and get anything to eat."

William looked at Septimus. They had not done any howling. They had not done any lurking, unless you counted five minutes down by the henhouse. William opened his mouth to tell the truth. But then Septimus gave him a big, special wink. It made William feel very grown up.

"That's right," he said. "What have you got, Mum? That howling is hard work. And as for lurking…"

"Of course it is," agreed Mrs Wolf. "Just sit down over there, both of you. I've got some lamb, two chickens and two little piglets I caught this morning."

She put the food on the table and Septimus tucked in. William looked down at his plate. He had a funny feeling in his tummy. It was hard to feel excited about his food. It wasn't the same now he had seen those sweet little lambs and fluffy chicks hopping about.

As usual, William said the first thing that came into his head.

"I think I'm going to be a…what's the word for it? One of those creatures that never eats meat – ever! Oh, I know – a vegetarian!"

There was a shocked silence. No one had ever said the word 'vegetarian' in Mrs Wolf's house before. Her eyes started to shine. Her lips started to curl.

"Is this the kind of thing that you teach your pupils, Mr Septimus Wolf?" she asked. "Exactly what has my son been learning from his lessons with you? William, tell me the truth. How much killing have you done in the past three weeks?"

"K-k-k-killing?" William was shocked. "Oh, Mum, I wouldn't dream of doing anything like that. It would be cruel. Don't you agree, Mr Septimus?"

The old wolf rolled his eyes. He held out his paws and shrugged his shoulders.

"Dear lady, what can I say? I have tried. Goodness knows, I have tried."

"Really?" Mrs Wolf's voice was getting

even colder. "William, how many animals have you seen Mr Septimus kill in the last three weeks?"

William shook his head. "Oh, Mum, I promise you, Mr Septimus doesn't do anything like that either," he said with a smile. "He doesn't even like chickens very much."

"That does surprise me," said Mrs Wolf. She looked down at the old wolf's empty plate. "I would have said he liked them very much. Now, Mr Septimus, I want my money back. You have not taught my William anything at all, except how to be a vegetarian."

But Septimus shook his head. "When a pupil can't even learn easy lessons, it is not the teacher's fault. I can't give you your money back."

"Then I shall have to write to the *Daily Growl* newspaper," said Mrs Wolf. "This

would make a very good story
for them. The famous
Septimus Wolf can't
even manage to
catch chickens!"

"More than
20 years of
ravaging and raging,
and this is the thanks I
get," cried the old wolf.
"So what if a wolf wants to take it easy in
his old age? Have a heart, Mrs Wolf!"

"Your mother ravaged and raged until
the day she died," snarled Mrs Wolf. "And
I think that she's the only one in your family
who did, Mr Septimus. There has always
been a lot of talk about you but, now I
come to think of it, I have never seen you
catch anything. It's all just talk! Leave my
house at once!"

William politely showed Septimus to

the door. Outside, the old wolf stopped and looked at him.

"Here's a useful piece of advice, my boy. Leave all that ravaging and raging to the girl wolves. They're much better at it than we are. Just do a bit of lurking and spread some scary stories about how nasty you are. You'll be fine, just like me."

The other day, I heard about a really nasty wolf over by the big hill. He goes by the name of William. The stories his mother tells about him would make your brains turn to jelly. She doesn't believe a word of them. But everyone else does, so Mrs Wolf is very proud of her famous son.

And as for William, he's very happy too. He spends most days playing with his best friend, Lily Lamb. And he is very proud of being the world's first ever vegetarian storybook wolf.

The Flying Football Boots

F red needed a new pair of football boots. His old ones were pinching his feet. "You've been growing as fast as a weed in the garden, Fred," his mum said, and she promised to take him to the sports shop to buy some new ones.

"I've scored loads of goals with these," Fred sighed, as he took off his beloved boots. He didn't tell anyone, but privately he felt sure that they were lucky boots that helped him play well.

"Would you mind if Sam had them?" asked Mum. "They're still quite new." Sam was Fred's little brother.

Fred was a bit worried. If Sam got his boots, would all the goal-scoring luck go to him instead?

But Fred wasn't a mean boy. Some children might have been grumpy about giving away their favourite boots, but he decided he didn't mind if his brother got some football luck. He, Fred, would just have to make some new luck with a brand-new pair of boots.

"Sure," he nodded.

"Good lad," replied his mum, smiling.

Fred and his mum went into town and began to walk towards a big sports shop full of new football kit.

"Let's go this way," Fred suggested, and pointed to a shortcut they didn't normally use. He didn't know why, but today he just felt it was the best way to go.

They walked down a tiny lane, too narrow for cars. The buildings on either side were old and squashed together. In one of them there was a small shop window no bigger than the window in Fred's bedroom at home.

"I don't remember seeing a shop along here before," Mum remarked, as they walked nearer.

"Look!" Fred cried, and stopped in his tracks.

Behind the dusty window there was a shelf with several pairs of funny-shaped odd-coloured shoes on it – they were not the kind of shoes that Fred had ever seen people wearing in his town. But in the middle of the shelf he saw the most fantastic pair of football boots he had ever set eyes on.

"Wow!" exclaimed Fred. He felt as if he'd found a hidden treasure. At first he thought the boots looked silver, but then they shimmered and seemed gold, and then he thought that perhaps they were a shiny blue. They seemed to change colour in the bright sunlight.

"Can I have those boots?" he begged his mum. "Pleeeeeeease!"

Inside, the shop was small and everything in it looked a bit crooked. Funnily enough, the owner was just the same – a small and crooked old man.

"Good day," he said in an old-fashioned way. Fred's mum asked if he could measure Fred's feet.

"He'd like a pair of boots like the ones in the window, if you have them in his size," she explained.

"Oh yes. No need to measure. They

will fit perfectly," the old man declared. He seemed to know Fred's shoe size. He picked out the pair from the window.

"Here are your boots," he said, as if they belonged to Fred already and the shop had just been looking after them.

It turned out they did fit Fred perfectly, and they were just the price his mum wanted to pay. The old man put the boots in a cardboard box with no writing on it. Then he put the box in a plain crackly paper bag, not at all like the shiny plastic ones that the big sports shop used.

As they left, the old man put his hand on Fred's shoulder.

"Enjoy your boots. You're a good lad," he murmured, which Fred thought was a weird thing to say, but quite friendly, too.

When Fred and his mum reached the end of the lane, Fred glanced back but couldn't see into the shop window any more. The old man had pulled down the blinds. He clearly didn't want any more customers that day.

As soon as Fred got home he put on his new boots and ran outside to practise some shots.

"Fred is going to take the free kick. He's brilliant!" Fred cried, pretending to be a TV commentator as he placed the ball on the grass. He walked back, turned and began to run towards the ball, aiming to kick it a long way. Only this time a very strange thing happened. As Fred ran, he started to lift off the ground, just like an aeroplane.

A very surprised Fred found himself looking down at his football from above. When he glanced at his boots he saw the reason. They had sprouted wings – feathery, silvery ones that flapped so hard they had lifted him into the air.

Fred felt scared. He put his arms out but that made him wobble and head towards a tree. But the boots seemed to know what to do. Their wings flapped harder and lifted him above the branches.

"I don't want to do this!" Fred squealed out loud.

The boots seemed to hear him. He immediately glided down and landed softly on the ground by his football.

Fred hesitated, not sure whether to move at all in case the boots began to fly again. But he noticed that the wings had disappeared. Slowly he sat down and carefully unlaced the boots. He took them off and carried them indoors. When Mum asked, "How are your new boots?" he muttered "Fine". But he wasn't at all sure about that.

"I need to experiment," Fred thought to himself. The next time he got a chance to go outside on his own he put his boots on, looked around to make sure nobody was watching, and then gave an order.

"Fly me over the roses," Fred whispered. The boots immediately sprouted wings and lifted him up over the flower-bed, setting him safely down on the other side.

"That's good. They obey me," Fred thought. He was going to be in control. He practised a few times more, asking the boots to fly him to different parts of the garden. Each time they did it safely and seemed to know how to avoid obstacles such as a tree branch or the garden shed.

Then Fred asked them to fly him up the street. This went smoothly enough, until suddenly his next-door neighbour, Mr Sykes, stepped out of his driveway. The boots swerved to avoid him, yet he never even glanced at Fred.

"Fly around Mr Sykes again," Fred ordered, curiously.

The boots flew him in a circle all the way around Mr Sykes, who acted as if Fred wasn't there.

"Set me down behind Mr Sykes," Fred ordered. The moment he was on the ground again, Mr Sykes turned and smiled. "Hello, Fred," he waved.

"Wow! I'm invisible when I fly!" Fred thought excitedly.

Back home Fred decided not to tell his secret. Mum might think that flying boots were too dangerous. But next time he tried them out he did wear his cycle helmet and knee pads, just in case he bumped into something.

As the days went by Fred got more daring with his flights. First, he plucked up the courage to fly over a crowded shopping mall. He swooped down really close to the shoppers and not one of them saw him. Then he tried flying up to a high statue in the middle of the town, and he sat on the top of it like a bird. One day he tried flying up the side of a tall office block, pretending to be Spiderman. But as soon as he reached the rooftop he looked down over the side and felt sick, so he didn't try that again.

Fred was saving his best idea for a very special place and time. His favourite football team would soon be playing a big match at the local football stadium. It was going to be played at night, and it was very expensive to buy tickets, so Fred knew he wouldn't normally be able to go. But with his flying boots, it could be different!

Fred went to bed on the night of the match with his bedroom window open. As soon as Mum had said goodnight, he slipped on his boots.

"Fly me to the football stadium," he whispered. The tiny silvery wings sprouted and lifted Fred gently out of the window into the warm night air.

He floated over buildings and above a busy road until he saw the stadium floodlights glowing like giant diamonds in the distance. The boots took Fred over the stadium roof and let him hover high above the pitch.

The crowd roared loudly as they watched the match. The players who ran around below him looked just like the little toy footballers that were lined up on Fred's windowsill at home.

"I could go down there," Fred thought

to himself, and his heart flipped at the idea.
Did he dare?

"Fly me down to the football game," he
whispered.

As he flew down the players grew
much bigger. He could hear them running
along, kicking the ball hard.

THWACK!

Occasionally they shouted to each
other:

"To me!"

"My ball!"

Fred weaved around
them, yet they couldn't
see him! There were
thousands of fans at
the game that night,
but not one of them
knew that Fred was
there.

The boots sped

Fred towards the goal alongside the forward players. They rushed him back as the other team threatened a goal. They even swooped him behind the goalkeeper as he made a save. Fred felt part of the action, as if he was on the team next to his heroes.

Then the referee blew his whistle to signal for a free kick, and that's when a really daring thought popped into Fred's mind. Could he...ought he...should he actually kick the ball?

Fred hovered behind the star player who was getting ready to take the kick. He whispered quickly to his boots:

"Let me score a goal."

The star player ran up to the ball.

Fred swooped in fast.

As the player swung his foot back to kick, so did Fred. He kicked the football a fraction of a second before the player and sent it flying into the net!

"Goal!"

The crowd went crazy.

The star player looked slightly puzzled, but the other players began to hug him and congratulate him for scoring. He soon forgot his odd feeling that he hadn't actually touched the ball.

Fred didn't mind people not knowing he was the real goal scorer. He was thrilled to have done it. His dream had come true, and later he flew home glowing with happiness.

After that memorable match Fred regularly became an invisible extra player on the pitch, helping his team but being careful to do so in a way that nobody would notice. Sometimes he left the match and flew near the manager, listening to him talking tactics. He occasionally flew up to the commentators' box and listened to them broadcasting on TV.

When the season ended, Fred's invisible hands helped to hold up the big silver cup that his team had won.

After the football season had finished, Fred tried flying to other parts of the town where he lived. But it wasn't nearly so exciting. So he put his boots away and waited for a new season to come around. But when it did, disaster struck.

Fred's feet had grown, and once again his boots were too small. Mum saw him struggling to put them on.

"Wiggle your toes. Let me see where they are," she said, and pressed down on the boot tips, where his toes were uncomfortably squashed up against the leather.

Then Mum uttered the dreaded words: "These boots are too small. You'd better give them to your little brother."

Fred was devastated. The boots were

really uncomfortable and, worse, when he tried them outside, they wouldn't fly. He sat in his bedroom and cried, but in his heart he knew what he had to do. The boots' magic was no good to him any more. He'd had his fun and now it was somebody else's turn.

Fred took the precious boots into his little brother's bedroom, and he told him their secret. He helped Sam to practise flying with them, and told him what fun he would have at the football stadium. When he watched the next match on TV he knew his little brother was there, on the pitch, having the time of his life.

Fred tried to find the shop where he'd bought the flying boots, but it had closed down. He knew the adventure was well and truly over for him when he saw its empty window.

But Fred was quite wrong about that.

The very next morning a mystery parcel arrived addressed to him. Inside there was a note that Fred read out loud: "Congratulations, Fred. You have won a competition for being a good and kind child."

"I didn't know you'd entered a competition," Mum remarked.

"Nor did I," Fred thought silently, and

he read on: "Your prize is a pair of international football boots for playing star football in stadiums around the world!"

Inside the parcel there was a pair of smart black football boots, which were exactly Fred's size.

Fred had an exciting thought. What if they were flying boots? Did this mean he could fly around the world to see football?

Yes, it did! With the new black boots Fred could journey across oceans and continents in the twinkling of an eye. Even better, he realized the boots could take him to watch the World Cup, which was about to be played.

Some amazing things happened during the World Cup matches later that year. Unbelievable goals were scored and astounding saves were made. When the World Cup was won, the players lifted it high and it was so heavy it wobbled and almost fell, but an unseen hand helped to hold it up safely.

Nobody noticed except for a small crooked old man who sat in the back of his dusty shoe shop. This old man knew magic, and he liked to use it to reward good kids who didn't get grumpy when they had to share their things with other children.

"Good lad, good lad," he murmured as he watched the World Cup being held up safely on TV.

It was almost as if he could see someone invisible on the screen.

Cows
Don't Do
the Splits!

J ason loved animals. He loved them as much as he loved people. He was sure that animals had feelings just the same as he did. They got hungry the same as he did, and tired, and thirsty, and hot and cold. He knew when his dog Rufus was happy because he wagged his tail so hard Jason thought he would wag it off. And he knew when Rufus was sad, because he put on a miserable face and went off on his own to be quiet.

The other thing Jason loved was drawing animals. He sat for hours at the kitchen table with his book of animals in front of him, as well as his big drawing pad and a packet of newly sharpened pencils.

Jason tried to draw a different animal every day. Some were easier to draw than others. He found the plump animals, like the hippopotamus and the elephant, were easier than the skinny ones, like the monkey. Jason wasn't often pleased with his drawings – the only one he really liked was the one he did of a bull. But Dad said to keep at it and one day he would be really good. So he did.

Jason lived in the countryside, where it was quiet and peaceful. During the summer holidays he cycled with friends, went fishing with Dad in the nearby river, went for walks with Rufus or sat at home drawing. He was never bored. But this holiday was going to be different. Three of his cousins were coming to stay.

"Two weeks," groaned Jason, when Mum told him. "But they hate it here. Last time they came they did nothing but moan."

"They're older now," said Mum. "It will be better this time."

"They're so stuck up," complained Jason.

Abigail, Jennifer and Giles lived in London. They liked doing very different things from Jason. Abigail spent most of her spare time learning ballet. She stood for hours in front of the long mirror in her bedroom. Dressed in her white tutu and pink ballet shoes, she would point her toes, raise her arms above her head and practise her curtsey. Abigail thought being a ballet dancer was just about the coolest thing in the world.

Jennifer wanted to be an actress. She went to stage school and put on plays at home with her brother and sister. She was always the star of the show and loved performing in front of her friends and family.

Giles was brainy. He spent a lot of time in the Science Museum in London. Like Jason, he was very interested in animals, but mainly extinct ones. He had a thing about dinosaurs. The one interest the children had in common with Jason was drawing. Giles liked drawing the dinosaur skeletons on display in the museum. Abigail liked drawing ballet dancers, and Jennifer liked painting pictures of flowers. The three children thought that they were pretty good artists.

They weren't looking forward to their holiday in the countryside.

"It'll be boring, boring, boring," moaned Abigail.

"I shall hate it," said Jennifer.

"Jason's okay, though," said Giles.

"Jason's okay," agreed Jennifer. "It's all those dribbling cows and sheep I can't stand."

"I think they're gross," said Abigail, sniffing.

However, when the cousins arrived at Jason's house they found there was something to interest them after all. The local paper was having a competition for the best children's drawing of a farmyard animal. The only rule was that it had to be drawn from life, not copied from a picture.

"It will be easy," said Giles, confidently. "Good job I've brought my drawing things."

"I've left mine at home," said Jennifer.

"So have I," said Abigail. She turned to

Jason. "Can you buy art materials in the country, Jason?" she asked, snootily.

Jason tried not to feel annoyed.

"Of course you can," he snapped.

The next day, the two girls went shopping and bought everything they needed. They were surprised to find the local art shop every bit as good as the one they used in London. In the afternoon they went to Willow Tree Farm to look at the animals. Mr Benson the farmer, who was one of the judges in the competition, was going to show them around and suggest an animal for each of them to draw.

"This is Patience," he said taking them into the cowshed. "You won't have any trouble drawing her. She knows how to stand still, does Patience. She can stand still till the cows come home!" He laughed loudly at his own joke.

The children smiled politely.

"Why is her nose running like that?" asked Abigail, pulling a face.

"Cows' noses always run," replied Farmer Benson.

"And what's that funny smell?"

"That's a cow smell," said Farmer Benson. "Nothing wrong with that."

Abigail wrinkled her small, rather dainty nose. "Why does she make so much noise when she eats?" she asked.

"You'll upset her with questions like that," said Farmer Benson. "Cows have feelings as well, you know."

Abigail looked at him impatiently.

"You have a go at drawing Patience," the farmer added. "It'll give you a chance to get to know her."

Next, Farmer Benson took them to the pigsty to see the pigs. His prize pig was called Ponsonby. Ponsonby was plump, muddy and a bit smelly. He was eating his dinner when they went in and didn't bother to look up.

"Pigs are very intelligent animals," Mr Benson told the children.

"My animal book says they're more intelligent than dogs," said Jason, reaching over to scratch the top of Ponsonby's head. The pig half closed his eyes. Eating and having his head scratched were two of his favourite things.

"If they are so intelligent, why can't

they keep themselves clean?" asked Jennifer. "He's covered in mud."

"That's how he keeps cool," replied the farmer.

"He's a disgusting eater!" went on Jennifer, listening to Ponsonby slurping.

Ponsonby lifted his head out of the trough and stared at Jennifer. She looked away. She didn't like the look in his little piggy eyes.

"You've annoyed him," laughed Farmer Benson, and he told Jennifer to draw Ponsonby.

Arthur the goat was pleased to see them. He was bored on his own. He came over to say hello and, without any warning, he snatched Giles's baseball cap out of his pocket and started to eat it.

"Hey!" shouted Giles, trying to snatch it back. Too late. Arthur swallowed hard and it was gone. He smacked his lips together with glee, and looked around for something else to eat. Giles was wearing a green T-shirt. Arthur liked green. He made a grab.

"Get off, you stupid beast!" said Giles.

Farmer Benson put his hands over Arthur's ears.

"Careful," he grinned. "He gets angry if you call him names." Mr Benson arranged for Giles to draw Arthur.

"That just leaves you, Jason," said the farmer. "Why don't you draw Big Horse?"

Jason was pleased. He and Big Horse were old friends. They had known each other a long time.

The next day the four children turned up at the farm with their drawing pads, pencils and easels. Each animal was in a separate stall and Farmer Benson had provided chairs for the children to sit on.

The pigsty had been cleaned out but

Jennifer still hated the smell. Wrinkling her nose, she looked for Ponsonby. At first she couldn't see him, and then she noticed him lying down in a corner.

"Get up, you lazy fat old pig!" she called rudely, resting her pad on the easel.

Ponsonby didn't move.

"Fat lazy old pig," repeated Jennifer. "Come closer, I can't draw you over there."

Ponsonby got up and came over, grunting. "That's more like it," said Jennifer. She studied the pig closely, picked up her pencil and drew a few lines on the pad. "If he keeps as still as this, I'll be finished in no time," she thought. Suddenly there was a flurry of movement followed by a series of grunts. Surprised, Jennifer looked up, Ponsonby had kicked his legs in the air and was standing on his head!

"Get down at once," ordered Jennifer. "I can't draw you doing a headstand!"

But Ponsonby wouldn't listen. Jennifer pleaded and shouted. She called him nasty names. She called him nice names. She cried and she begged, but Ponsonby refused to move.

Giles was having a similar problem. Arthur insisted on doing cartwheels round and round the goat shed, until Giles felt giddy watching him.

In the cowshed, Abigail's drawing was

going well. Patience was behaving perfectly. She stood very still with her head turned to one side. It was the perfect position. Abigail studied her carefully and started to draw. She drew her head. She drew her body and she drew her tail.

Suddenly, Patience stuck two legs out to the right and two legs out to the left and sank slowly to the ground. Patience could do the splits!

Abigail's mouth opened with amazement, but no sound came out. Patience fluttered her long eyelashes, and she stayed doing the splits until Abigail had left the cowshed.

When the children had finished they gave their drawings to Farmer Benson. To their relief, he didn't look at them. "We'll be judging in a week's time," he told them.

Jason's cousins didn't say anything to each other, or to anyone else, about how the animals had behaved for them. They were very quiet that evening and didn't want to do very much. Jason's mother was surprised when they went to bed just after eight o'clock.

The day came when everyone who had entered the competition gathered in the town hall to find out which drawing had won. The judges were on a stage at the front of the hall, with a huge pile of drawings spread out in front of them.

"We are pleased to say that the standard of drawing this year is very high," said one of the judges.

"Yes," said another, "the drawings are so good that it has been difficult to choose a winner."

"But in the end we all agreed on one that we thought was better than the rest." The judges looked around at the eager faces.

"But first," said a judge, "there are three drawings in particular that we want to mention. We all thought these drawings were most unusual, and all three are unsigned." One of the judges held up a drawing. Giles recognized his drawing of Arthur.

"Have any of you ever seen a goat doing cartwheels?" asked the judge. "Goats don't do cartwheels!" he added.

The audience laughed. Giles felt his face burning with shame.

Then the judge held up another drawing for everyone to see. "And what about this one?" he said. "Pigs don't do headstands!"

It was Jennifer's turn to go red.

"AND COWS DON'T DO THE SPLITS!" he added, holding up Abigail's drawing.

The audience laughed.

"Will the three children who did these come up on the stage please?" asked one of the judges. Abigail, Giles and Jennifer got to their feet. None of them spoke, but each silently wished they had been nicer to the animals at Mr Benson's farm. If only they had shown them a little more respect, this wouldn't have happened.

When they got up on stage, they were surprised to see that all three judges were smiling. "We have decided to award you the second, third and fourth prizes," said one of them, "for the three most original drawings." And he shook the three of them by the hand.

The children couldn't believe their ears. In the audience Jason and his mother were clapping loudly.

"And the winner of the competition,

with his excellent drawing of Big Horse," went on the judge, "is Jason."

The audience cheered and clapped as loudly as they could. But none clapped louder than Giles, Abigail and Jennifer. Grinning broadly, Jason walked onto the stage to collect his prize. He hugged each of his cousins and they hugged him back. They were beginning to look at Jason with a new respect and admiration.

As for Jason, the next time his cousins came to stay he didn't mind at all. They had much more in common now, and did lots more things together.

And never again did Giles, Abigail and Jennifer take animals' feelings for granted. From now on they always made sure they treated them the same way as they liked to be treated themselves.

Music or Magic?

Harvey had to decide which subjects he was going to study at school next term. He had one more choice to make. But he didn't know which subject would be best. So he asked his father to help him. Mr Baker looked at the list of subjects.

"Geology, geography, maths, music and magic," he read out loud. "Well, of course you should choose maths."

"No, Dad, I already chose maths," said Harvey. "Look! I knew you wouldn't let me drop that. Anyway, I quite like it, in an odd sort of way."

"Accountants are not odd," grinned Mr Baker. "OK, let's think about this. What are the other choices? You've already chosen geography. How about geology?"

"I don't really want to do geology," said Harvey. "It's taught by Miss Matthews, and she really *is* odd."

"Well, that only leaves two choices," said his father. "Music or magic? Wait a minute, music or magic? Magic? Since when was magic a school subject?"

"There's a new teacher called Mr Izard," Harvey replied. "He's going to be teaching it, but I don't know what it means. I suppose it's card tricks or pulling rabbits out of hats, that sort of thing."

"Well, that settles it!" Mr Baker was frowning. He didn't like the sound of cards and rabbits. "Anything called 'magic' has to be a waste of time. You'll have to do music."

Harvey nodded. He knew that he was not very good at music. He always made the wrong noises with the instruments. And he didn't like Mr Alvis, the music teacher. But there was no way his father was going to let him do something called 'magic'. Harvey filled in his form and got his dad to sign it at the bottom. Then he posted it back to school.

Harvey really meant to work hard and do his best at music. But when he was standing outside the music-room door, he stopped. He could hear the wailing and screeching coming from inside. He could imagine himself trying to play the violin. And he suddenly couldn't bear the thought any more. Harvey ran away from the music room and out to the huts behind the school. That was where the magic classes were being held.

Harvey thought the classroom would be full of children. But it was almost empty. The only person in the room was a tall thin man. He was standing at the front of the room, writing something strange on the board. He turned around as Harvey walked in.

"I'm Mr Izard," he said. "You must be Harvey."

Mr Izard was a strange-looking man. He had white hair and a long, droopy white moustache. He was wearing a pair of bright green trousers and a lemon-coloured shirt, with a polka-dot necktie.

"Have I got the time wrong?" asked Harvey. "Why is no one else here yet?"

"No, you've got the time right," said Mr Izard. "You're the only pupil doing magic this term. It's going to be just you and me. We will be able to do a lot more work with only the two of us. A big class of 30 never gets past Chapter Four of *The Spellbinder's Handbook* in a term. We shall probably finish it and start on Book Two."

"Are we going to be learning card tricks?" asked Harvey.

"Nonsense!" cried Mr Izard. "I am going to teach you some wonderful things, Harvey. You don't really want to learn card tricks, do you? You just said that to your dad. You always hoped for spells, didn't you? They are so much more interesting than pulling rabbits out of hats (the rabbits don't like it either)."

Harvey nodded. He liked Mr Izard already.

"Do I need to talk?" he asked. "I mean, you can tell what I'm thinking anyway…"

"Clever boy! You're getting the hang of this already," laughed Mr Izard. "But I think it is better if we do talk. You can fall into bad habits otherwise. What if we were at lunch one day, and I thought 'Pass the salt!' and you did it without me saying anything? People might think it was odd."

"Would that matter?" asked Harvey. He thought it would be good fun to read people's minds.

"Another good question! Should magic be kept secret or shared with everyone? What do you think, Harvey?"

"I think it should be shared," said Harvey. "It's not fair if you don't pass on good ideas you find out about. It's mean and selfish."

Mr Izard sat down and put his chin on his hands. His eyes twinkled.

"Once upon a time, when I was young, then I might have agreed with you, Harvey," he said. "But I've learned my lesson. Sometimes it's better not to tell people about magic. But it's up to you. I don't suppose your father will mind very much that you're not doing music, will he?"

"Oh!" Harvey had forgotten about that. He knew his father would stop the magic lessons if he found out about them. And now Harvey had met Mr Izard, he wanted to do magic more than ever.

"Maybe it would be best if I learn a bit of magic first," he said. "When I do tell people about it, I can do something magic to show them. They might not laugh or be cross then."

"I think that's a very good plan," said Mr Izard. "Now, let's start work."

Harvey still wasn't sure what he was going to learn. You can't *really* learn magic, can you? But that is exactly what he did. Soon he knew how to turn on the lights without moving out of his chair. He could get dressed in a second, too. He learned how to tidy his room and do the washing-up, all with a wave of his hand. It was very useful.

Mr Baker didn't ask Harvey anything about his new lessons. He would only be

interested in the tests at the end of term.

But, as a matter of fact, Harvey's schoolwork was going really well. He found that a little bit of magic made his homework very, very easy.

His English teacher was very pleased when she saw that Harvey's handwriting was neater. She didn't know that he had watched his essay being written by his pen.

His geography homework was finished in five minutes after he cast a spell on his felt-tip pens.

His maths homework was easy – he just let his pencil do the sums.

In the end, Harvey didn't have to do any work at all. He had the best term ever. But, on the Friday before the end-of-term tests were due to start, Mr Izard gave him a terrible shock.

"Looking forward to the tests on Monday, Harvey?" he asked.

"I'm not bothered, really," said Harvey.

"Done lots of revision, have you? Good lad."

"Well, no!" Harvey looked surprised. "I'm just going to use a bit of magic to do the tests. It works really well for my homework."

Mr Izard suddenly looked very, very

serious.

"I'm very sorry to hear that, Harvey," he said. "I had no idea. No idea at all."

"About what? What's the matter?" Harvey was starting to feel a cold and horrible feeling in his stomach. Mr Izard's next words made the feeling even colder.

"You're not supposed to use magic to help yourself," said the teacher. "Surely I told you that in the first lesson?"

"I don't think so," said Harvey. He was feeling very scared.

"Really? Well, that's a pity. But facts are facts. You cannot use magic to help yourself. If another magician catches you doing it, he has to stop you. So I will have to stop you from using any kind of spell in your exams. Illifillifoop! There, it's done."

Harvey felt a strange, tickling feeling go down his back. He knew that Mr Izard had cast a spell on him. He would not be able to use magic in the tests. He stared at his teacher. Suddenly, Mr Izard didn't seem like such a nice and interesting person. Harvey had the feeling that he had been tricked. He frowned.

"But you taught me how to turn on lights without touching the switch," he said. "You showed me how to get dressed in one second. That's using magic to help yourself!"

"Not if you're a doctor rushing out to see a sick patient," said Mr Izard. "Of course, you are only meant to use the spells in an emergency. I can't believe you would be so silly as to use them for everyday life."

"But you didn't tell me not to!" Harvey cried.

"Harvey, you're not a stupid boy!" snapped Mr Izard. He looked quite cross. "Didn't you feel a little bit guilty? After all, you did it in secret, didn't you? You didn't tell anyone else about the magic you learned."

Harvey was angry now.

"You tricked me!" he shouted. "I'm going to tell the headmaster. You can't be allowed to do this!"

Harvey ran to

the headmaster's office. But he didn't knock on the door. What was he going to say? Harvey decided that there were better things he could be doing. He could start to read the textbooks he hadn't looked at all term. He had only two days to learn a whole term's work!

Harvey worked hard all weekend. But he had spent so long using magic, that he had forgotten lots of really easy things. It was hard to write with a pen in the old-fashioned way. It was hard to do sums in his head. He tried to read all his textbooks, but it was no use. There just wasn't enough time.

Harvey was pale and tired when he sat down in the classroom on Monday morning. When he looked at the first test, he got a sick feeling in his stomach. He didn't know the answer to a single question.

It was an awful week. The tests just got worse and worse. In the last test he answered only one question. Harvey knew that he had done very badly indeed. He felt terrible. Even Mr Baker noticed that something was wrong.

"You've been working too hard," he said. "Let's go away on a trip. We could go fishing now that term is over. It doesn't matter if your results have to wait until we get back."

"No, another week won't matter," agreed Harvey. "OK! Let's go fishing."

But he knew that he was only putting it off. Harvey had always got good results at school. His father loved to boast about how well he was doing. What on earth was he going to say when the results came through this time? Harvey felt as if he never wanted to hear the word 'magic' again.

While they were away, Harvey kept trying to tell his father about the terrible mistake he had made.

"Dad, about the tests," he said, "I wanted to say…"

But his father just said: "Shhhhh! You'll disturb the fish!" Or he shook his head and said: "It's time to forget about all that, Harvey. Let's just enjoy ourselves."

It's not easy to enjoy yourself when you know that something bad is going to happen. It was the worst week Harvey had ever spent. It was even worse than the week of the tests.

When they got home there was a pile of envelopes on the doormat. Harvey saw the envelope from the school straight away. He picked it up, but he couldn't open it.

"Mind if I look?" asked Mr Baker.

Harvey closed his eyes and handed the envelope to his father.

He heard the envelope being opened.

There was a long, long silence.

Then Mr Baker gave a loud cheer!

"Top marks in everything, Harvey. Well done! These are the best results you've ever had! And look, I knew you'd be good at music. You'll have to tell me what you've been doing. What's your favourite instrument?"

Harvey just opened and closed his mouth. He looked a bit like a goldfish. Mr

Baker grinned at him. "There's another letter for you here," he said.

Harvey's dad handed him a large lemon-yellow envelope with green writing on it. The writing was very thin and spidery.

Harvey opened the envelope carefully. When he read the letter inside, it explained rather a lot:

Dear Harvey,

I felt a bit guilty about tricking you in our magic lessons. It wasn't a very kind thing to do. I hope I made it up to you by helping out with your exams. You can't do magic to help yourself. But you can use it to help another magician.

I've decided that teaching isn't really for me. I won't be there when you go back next term. No one will be able to remember me at all. You will be doing geology instead. You'll be a term behind, so you will have to work hard!

I hope you learned a lot this term, Harvey, and not just about magic.

Best wishes

W. Izard

Harvey gave a big smile. He folded up the letter and hid it under his pillow. Magic was useful after all. Perhaps one day he might even take magic lessons again. But right now he had work to do – he had to catch up on a whole term of geology!

Maisy's Big Mission

One day a stranger arrived in Bluebell Wood. She introduced herself to a friendly magpie.

"I'm Betty, the brown owl. Do you know this wood well?" she asked.

"Well, I know the south side of it because that's where I live. I'm Maisy, by the way," the magpie replied.

"Perhaps you could help me," Betty said. "I'd like to move to this wood and build a nest, but I must have peace and quiet. I sleep during the day, you see. I can't bear to be woken up in daylight."

"It sounds as if you need to go to the north side of the wood. Nobody lives there and it's very quiet. Are you sure you'd like it? The south side is so much livelier."

Maisy didn't mind noise. The livelier a place was, the better she liked it. In fact, Maisy's favourite pastime was to leave the wood and visit the busy local street. There she would perch on a handy fence in front of the TV shop. She would ignore the traffic rumbling by and the shoppers chattering away, and she would settle down to watch the lovely moving pictures on the TV screens in the shop window. That wouldn't do at all for Betty. It sounded far too noisy.

"My nerves would never stand it," twittered Betty.

Betty flew to the north side of the wood and chose a place to build her nest. It was a calm spot, and nobody else lived nearby. At least, Betty thought that she was alone until Ratso Rat arrived at the foot of her tree.

"Hey, lady. Are you sure you want to

move in around here?" he called up to her.

"Oh, do I know you?" Betty replied sniffily.

"Ratso's the name. I live here, on the north side, so if you're really going to stay we'll be neighbours. But, if I were you, I wouldn't live here because..." he began.

"I am perfectly happy, thank you," Betty cut him off because she was very irritated by him. She didn't want to share the north side of the wood with anyone else.

"Suit yourself, lady," Ratso replied. He twitched his whiskers and scampered off.

The next day, Maisy visited Betty to see how she was settling in. Betty complained to her about Ratso.

"Oh yes, I forgot about him. I don't really know him," Maisy explained. "He's probably OK but he keeps himself to himself. He does his own thing."

"Well, I shall do the same," Betty

declared. "And my 'thing' is not to talk to rats. But there is something else I am worrying about. Now I've had a chance to look around properly I've seen a building nearby. Look over there."

Sure enough, beyond the edge of the wood they could see the roof of a building. Maisy didn't know anything about it, being from the south side.

"That's new," Maisy remarked. "Is it noisy?"

"Not at all. It seems to be empty,"

Betty explained.

"Oh well, that's all right then," Maisy told the nervous owl.

The days went by and Betty was happy with her new home. She slept peacefully during the day and hunted at night. The nearby building was no trouble to her. Her only other neighbour, Ratso, didn't bother to visit either. She felt so comfortable that she laid some eggs in her new nest.

Unfortunately there was something very important that Betty didn't know, and nor did Maisy. The building was a brand-new school. It was only quiet because it was the school holidays.

The awful truth came out when the new term began. One morning, Betty was awoken by the sound of chattering parents bringing their children into the playground.

"Hello!"

"How are you!"

"Hi there!" they cried loudly to each other.

"What? Oh my goodness!" Betty woke with a jump.

Once the children had gone inside she dozed off again, but soon it was breaktime. The shouting and the laughing began again, only this time with something worse. Every now and again one of the teachers would come into the playground and blow a whistle to get the children's attention.

The whistle really upset Betty. She complained bitterly to Maisy next time the magpie visited.

"The noise goes right through my head!" she wailed. "Oh, it's terrible! I think I could learn to cope with the voices, but not the whistle!"

"But surely they don't use it very much, do they?" asked Maisy.

"They do!" exclaimed Betty. "The

teachers use it all day – at breaktime, lunchtime and even in the afternoon during PE. Oh, Maisy. I'm exhausted!"

As they chatted, Ratso appeared below Betty's tree.

"I see the school's opened," he shouted up to them.

"Did you know it was a school?" Maisy asked him.

"Of course I did. I used to go over and steal the workmen's sandwiches when they were building it. It doesn't bother me," he said.

"Why didn't you tell me?" Betty gasped.

"I tried to, lady, but you didn't seem to want to chat to a rat," said Ratso, and disappeared before she could reply.

"I can't move now," Betty groaned. "I must look after my eggs. I shall have to put up with it."

Poor old Betty found it even harder as

the days went by. Whenever she dozed off, the whistle woke her up. When evening came she was too exhausted to go hunting. She began to look thin and ill.

"This is an emergency. You need help," Maisy declared. "Don't panic, Betty. I'll get the other woodland animals to help. We'll mount a mission. You stay here. I'm going to get my team ready!"

Maisy flew back to the south side of the wood, where her other friends lived.

First, she called on Sonny the squirrel.

"You have great skills. I need you for a top-secret mission. Will you help?" she begged.

"Er, all right," Sonny agreed. He thought she was playing some sort of game.

Next they called on Sally, a small and timid sparrow.

"I need you on a top-secret mission. Follow me," Maisy ordered, and didn't give Sally the chance to say "No".

As the trio reached the north side of the wood, Ratso appeared in their path.

"Hello. What's this? A gang?" he chuckled.

"We're going on a mission to save Betty from the school's whistle. We're going to steal it," Maisy declared.

"Are we?" Sonny and Sally gasped in panic.

"Join us, Ratso," Maisy suggested.

"No thanks," Ratso shook his head. "Why should I help that grumpy old owl? It's obvious she doesn't like rats. I think I'll just watch you lot. It should be very funny."

"Suit yourself, if you're too scared to join us," Maisy replied. She stalked off, followed by a very worried Sonny and Sally.

"First, we need to collect information," Maisy announced. This meant they had to creep to the edge of the wood and watch the comings and goings in the playground.

"Look! The teacher has the whistle on a ribbon round her neck," Maisy whispered.

"How in hazelnuts are we going to get THAT?" Sonny asked.

"I don't know yet. Let me think," Maisy insisted.

Once the children went inside for lessons, the animals crept into the empty playground. They noticed the same teacher standing inside the staffroom.

"Look! she's taking the whistle off and hanging it on a hook," Maisy cried excitedly. Then the teacher went out, leaving the staffroom empty.

"This is the plan," Maisy whispered. "Sonny, when the front door opens you go inside the school to get the whistle. We'll stay outside and keep a lookout."

"That's not fair! I'm not going on my own!" Sonny squeaked.

"But you're good at creeping around and climbing. You can climb up and get the whistle without being seen," said Maisy.

"I'll only go if you come with me," Sonny insisted.

"But I'm far too big to go into school unnoticed. Sally, you go!" Maisy ordered.

"B...b..but," Sally spluttered.

"Quick! The front door's opening!" Maisy cried. "Good luck, team!"

The door opened and someone came

out. Before it swung shut Sonny dashed through, with Sally hopping nervously behind.

Maisy waited and watched through the staffroom window for what seemed like hours. Teachers came in and out but there was no sign of Sonny and Sally. Had they managed to get into the staffroom?

Luckily, they had. When the room became empty again Maisy saw Sonny leap up on the table, followed by Sally.

"Good. Now all they have to do is climb up and get the whistle," Maisy muttered to herself. Unfortunately, her top emergency rescue team did neither of these things. The greedy pair were distracted by a plate of biscuits on the staffroom table. Sonny and Sally had begun to nibble at the crumbs, unable to resist them.

Maisy hopped up and down, squawking angrily. "Get on with it!" she cried.

Sonny looked up. He glanced at the whistle on its ribbon, as if he was finally about to make an attempt to get it, but then disaster struck. The staffroom door flew open and a teacher walked in.

Sonny and Sally bolted under the table. The teacher didn't see them, but Maisy knew it was only a matter of time. They were both in terrible danger!

"Oops. That's a sticky situation," Ratso whispered behind Maisy's back. He had been watching all along.

"Oh dear. What can I do? This wasn't

supposed to happen. It's all gone wrong," Maisy wailed, as more teachers came into the staffroom and sat around the table. She imagined Sonny hoping that nobody would stand on his tail. As for poor Sally, her tiny heart would be thumping hard.

"I guess you'll be wanting some fearless hero to rescue them," Ratso sighed, casually stroking his whiskers.

"Oh yes! But who?" Maisy cried desperately.

"I s'pose I'll have to do it," Ratso said.

"Ratso!" Maisy gasped. "Yes! Join the mission! You need to go in through the front door as soon as it opens. Then hurry round to the staffroom door..."

Ratso shook his head.

"I'll do it my way, lady," he murmured. He ran off and scrambled up a tree, then along a branch, before bounding onto the school roof. He scampered along it and took a flying leap across a gap onto another section of roof.

"He's like super-rat!" Maisy declared.

Ratso reached the top of a drainpipe and disappeared inside it. Minutes later he reappeared in the staffroom, just as the teachers were leaving. Maisy had no idea at all how he had managed to get inside.

Ratso climbed up a coat that was hanging near the whistle, swung from its sleeve and grabbed the whistle ribbon between his teeth. He pulled it off its hook and ran back down.

Maisy saw Sonny and Sally hop out from their hiding place. Then the gang gathered on the table, discussing what to do next.

Maisy couldn't believe what she saw next. All three of them started tucking into the biscuits again!

"Get out!" Maisy cried, but Ratso just

glanced at her through the window, looking completely cool and relaxed as he munched on a biscuit. He seemed to be waiting for something.

Then a teacher opened the staffroom door once more. Ratso turned around and stood up on his hind legs to give her a good view of him. The teacher screamed loudly and flung her hands in the air. It was the signal for the gang to race out through the door.

Clever Ratso had planned it all along!

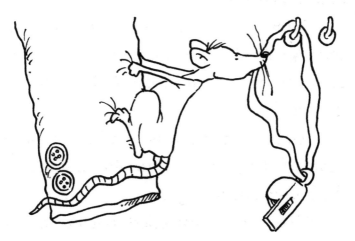

He knew humans hated to see rats, and he had counted on the teacher panicking and allowing them to escape. All they'd had to do was sit on the table and wait for someone to come in.

Ratso must have showed himself inside the school corridor, too, because Maisy heard more screams and then the front door was flung open. Sally came flying out, followed by Sonny scampering as fast he could. Behind them came Ratso, carrying the whistle in his mouth with the ribbon flying behind. They didn't stop until they reached the safety of Bluebell Wood.

The teacher was convinced she had seen more than one rat in the staffroom that day. In fact, the more she thought about it, the more rats she imagined. Soon a high fence was built between the school and the wood to keep out any 'nasty animals'. The school never did buy a new

whistle, and instead the teachers just clapped to get the pupils' attention. Betty got used to that and slept through it.

When Betty heard the story of Ratso's bravery she apologized for being so rude to him. Ratso became the woodland hero, but he insisted he'd done nothing special.

"I just did my rat thing," he replied if anyone praised him. When Maisy asked how he got into the school he wouldn't tell.

"We rats have our secrets," he winked mysteriously. He gave the whistle to Maisy because magpies love shiny things. But he made her promise not to mount any more missions without asking him first.

"If you need help, call me, lady," he said.

Maisy stopped watching TV action movies after that. "They're just not very true to life," she told Betty. "I've seen the real thing, and I know that proper action heroes have whiskers!"

The Ghost Tree

A long time ago, Hopeville was a very busy town. It was built on top of a diamond mine. So there were lots of very rich people. All the rich people lived in a place called Haversham Gardens.

There were big houses with white pillars around the doors in Haversham Gardens. There were huge lawns with tall trees. There were servants in white gloves to welcome visitors. Rich people built the houses and rich people lived there.

But then the diamond mine ran out of diamonds. So the mine owners closed the mine. The rich people left the town. The big houses started to fall down and the gardens became overgrown.

A little boy called Matthew lived in Hopeville with his mother and his grandfather. Hopeville was a very quiet place now. But Matthew loved it.

One day Matthew was playing by the river when he found a strange stone in the rocky bank. He took it home to show his mother, but she didn't know what it was. Then he showed it to his grandfather. Grandpa jumped up and down and waved his hands in the air.

"Calm down, Dad!" said his daughter. "What are you trying to say?"

It was a long time since the old man had done any jumping up and down. It took him ten minutes to get his breath back.

"It's a diamond!" he panted at last. "It's a great big beautiful diamond!"

Matthew and his mother gasped.

"It can't be," said Matthew's mum. "It doesn't look like a diamond at all. It's rough and it's not sparkly."

"That's what they're like at first!" cried Grandpa. "They have to be cut and polished to look like jewels. I tell you, this is a *real* diamond. I should know – I worked in the diamond mine when I was younger."

Matthew looked at the diamond. He was pleased that he had found it.

Grandpa smiled. "Do you know what this means?" he asked. "You and your mother are rich now. And the old mine will be opened up. There'll be life in this old town again."

"But I didn't find it in the old mine," Matthew said. "I found it by the river."

"Well, someone should start digging there right away," said Grandpa. "Where there's one diamond, there may be more! I'll just go and get my spade…"

But Matthew's mother put her hand on his arm.

"Oh no, you don't," she said. "You are much too old for that kind of thing. We'll ring up the mine company. Let them do the digging. If what you say is true, we've got plenty right here in my hand!"

And so Matthew and his mother sold their big diamond to the mining company. But it was hard to decide what to do with the money they received.

"What do you think we should do, Grandpa?" asked Matthew.

"All my life, I've dreamed of living in Haversham Gardens," said Matthew's grandfather. "Let's go and live there now."

"But those houses are in ruins," said his daughter. "And they're so dark and gloomy."

"But it's what I've always wanted," said Grandpa. "I want to grow pumpkins, so I need a big garden. And the biggest gardens are in Haversham Gardens."

"I suppose they are the nicest houses in Hopeville," said Matthew's mother. "And we have enough money to repair one. Let's see what's for sale."

It turned out that the biggest house of all, Maple Villa, was for sale. The house was in a very bad state, and its garden was like a jungle, but the family decided to buy it. They thought it would be fun to make it look beautiful again.

Matthew went up to the house to look around. He wasn't allowed inside while all the building work was going on. But he was allowed to walk around the garden. It was a wonderful place to play and explore. In the middle of the garden, there was a very tall maple tree. And its branches were perfect for climbing.

Matthew went up to the house every day after school. He spent his afternoons sitting in the branches of the big tree, swinging his legs. When he had been going there for a while, something odd happened. He started to have a funny feeling that the tree was talking to him.

Maybe you are wondering how a tree can talk to a human being. It was very odd. In a way, it wasn't like talking. Matthew didn't hear a voice. It was just that he suddenly knew things that no one else had told him anything about. It was as if the tree had just put them into his memory.

The first time it happened was one evening at supper. Matthew had spent all afternoon sitting in the maple tree. He had been reading one of his library books. His mother and grandfather were talking about their new home.

"I wonder who lived there first," said his mother. "I'd love to know more about the history of the house. It is so beautiful. I bet it has lots of stories to tell."

Matthew suddenly found he knew the answer. "It was the Ramsays who lived there first," he said. "Mr Ramsay was the manager of the first mine. He was a big, tall man with a beard. His wife was small with black hair. They had thirteen children but only six of them lived to grow up. That used to happen a lot in those days. Mr Ramsay died when he fell off his horse on the way home from the mine one day."

Matthew's mother and grandfather looked at him in surprise.

"That's amazing! Where did you find out all that?" asked his mother.

"I didn't," Matthew said.

"Yes, but you just told us!" laughed Grandpa. "You must have read it somewhere. Did you learn it in a history lesson? Or find a book in the library?"

But Matthew shook his head. "I don't know how I know," he said. "I suppose I must have read it somewhere." He didn't even think about the tree.

The next time it happened was at school. The teacher asked the class to write a mystery story.

"It could be a real-life mystery that will never be solved," she said. "Or it might be something you make up yourself."

Some children didn't know what to write about. But Matthew started writing straight away.

"Mr Ramsay of Maple Villa died when he fell off a horse," he wrote. "He left behind a wife and six children. The eldest son was called Tom. He decided to go off and seek his fortune.

"Tom went abroad. At first he wrote lots of letters. But then his letters stopped coming. Everyone thought he was dead. The second son was called John. When his mother died, he got married and lived in Maple Villa. He became the manager of the mine, just like his father. He was one of the most important men in town. But he was a bad man."

Matthew chewed his pen. Then he started writing even more quickly than before. "John was the richest man in Hopeville. He thought he was too good to talk to the ordinary people in the town.

"One winter's night, there was a knock at the door. John's maid went to open it. She saw a rough-looking man with long hair and a beard. The maid thought he was a tramp and told him to go away. But the man ignored her. He walked into the house. 'This is my home,' he said. 'Is my mother here? Tell her Tom has come home!'"

The teacher was reading over Matthew's shoulder.

"That's a great story," she said. "But I wanted you to write a mystery story. Where is the mystery?"

"The mystery is what happened to Tom," Matthew replied. "After that night, he was never seen again. The servants were suddenly sent to new jobs hundreds of miles away. The Ramsays became even more snooty than before. And no one in the town ever heard that Tom had come back."

Matthew finished writing his story. The teacher was very pleased with him. She read his story to the whole class.

"Matthew has a wonderful imagination," she said. "How did you come to think of this story?"

"Oh," said Matthew, "I didn't make it up. All of it is true. Someone – I can't remember who – told it to me."

"But in the story, you wrote that all the servants were sent away. No one in the town knew about Tom. So how could anyone have told you?" asked the teacher.

"I don't know," said Matthew. "And I don't really know what happened to Tom. But I can guess. I don't think John wanted him to come home."

After school, Matthew went up to Maple Villa as usual. He climbed into the tree and sat on a branch, swinging his legs. When he had been sitting there for an hour, he gave a big sigh. Suddenly he knew what had happened to Tom. It wasn't a very nice story. Matthew shivered and climbed down from the tree.

That night, Matthew talked to his mother. "I don't think we should move to Maple Villa," he said. "I don't want to live

in a house where there's been a murder."

"A murder? Don't be silly," laughed his mother. "There hasn't been a murder at Maple Villa. We'd have heard about it.

We've lived in this town all our lives. Grandpa has been here even longer. There's never been any story of a murder up at Maple Villa. Where did you hear such a tale?"

This time, Matthew knew the answer. "The tree told me," he said. "It tells me secrets. I sit in the old maple tree in the middle of the garden. After a while, I just know things."

"Your imagination is running away with you, my lad," said his grandfather. "Time for bed, I think, before you have any more odd ideas."

But next morning, Matthew's mother got an important phone call. Matthew saw her face go white. She put the phone down and looked at Matthew and Grandpa.

"That was the builders," she said. "They've called the police. They have found a skeleton in the cellar of Maple Villa.

What could it mean? I hope there's a good reason why it's there."

But there are not many good reasons why you would find a skeleton in your cellar. The police found a cross next to the skeleton. There was a name on the cross – it said 'Tom Ramsay'. When Matthew's mother heard that, she looked at Matthew.

"Just like your story," she said.

"Just like the tree told me," nodded Matthew.

Matthew's mother was a very sensible woman. She decided to find out if the tree really did tell secrets. She borrowed a ladder from the builders and went down to the garden. Matthew helped his mother and his grandfather climb up into the tree. Then he climbed up behind them. They all sat in a row on the biggest branch, and waited to see what the tree had to say.

Matthew's mother was worried.

Should they still move into the house, now that they knew about the terrible thing that had happened to Tom Ramsay?

Matthew was worried. Would he lose his friends if he moved into such a grand house?

Matthew's grandfather was worried. What if Matthew and his mother did not want to move? Where would he grow his pumpkins?

They sat on the branch for a long time. Then Matthew's mother started to smile. After a while, Matthew and his grandfather started to smile too.

"The tree says that the house needs a good family to live here again," Matthew's mother said. "It says that I will meet a wonderful man and have five more sons!"

"The tree told me that the patch next to the house is just right for growing pumpkins," chuckled Grandpa. "It said I'm going to win the pumpkin prize at the fruit and vegetable show for the next ten years!"

"The tree says that I'm going to be school football captain," said Matthew. He looked very pleased.

"That's decided, then," said Matthew's mother. "We will move into Maple Villa as soon as the building work is done."

The family stayed in the tree until late in the afternoon. Then they climbed down and walked back to their old home in

Hopeville. They all felt very excited.

That was ten years ago. Nowadays, the family in Maple Villa is very happy.

Matthew's grandfather works hard in his pumpkin patch every day. He has won lots and lots of prizes.

Matthew's mother loves her house and they have lots of visitors.

Matthew is almost grown up. But he still loves to sit in the maple tree – when he can keep his five little brothers out of it!

Knock, Knock! Who's There?

"Get off me, you silly dog!" hissed Joe Burns, trying to keep his voice down. He was crouched on the floor while a little black-and-white dog jumped all over him.

"Get off me," hissed Joe again. "Get off!"

But the dog took no notice. He leaped on Joe's back and licked the inside of his ear.

"Stop it!" snarled Joe. But the dog wouldn't stop. He thought Joe's ear tasted pretty good.

Joe was trying to keep as quiet as he could. He didn't want anyone to know where he was. Joe was in Kevin Bean's house and he was not supposed to be there. Joe was a burglar!

The dog licked Joe's other ear, then he licked his nose. He was only a little dog, a puppy really, and he wanted to be friends with everyone. He especially wanted to be friends with Joe.

Joe sat on the floor with the puppy in his arms and hoped that no one had heard him. Slowly he got to his feet and switched on his torch. He was in a sort of passageway. The house was very quiet. Breathing a sigh of relief, Joe put the puppy down. Then he heard a scrabbling sound at the front door. A cat, carrying a mouse, shot in through the cat flap. When the cat saw Joe, it dropped the mouse, and the mouse ran up Joe's trouser leg.

Chaos followed.

"Aaagh!" said Joe, clutching at his leg. The cat tried to get at the mouse and tripped up Joe. As he fell, Joe dropped the torch, which went out. The puppy jumped on Joe and started barking. Then he began licking again, and for the second time that night Joe's ears and nose were given a really good clean.

After a while the puppy stopped. Joe felt his leg. The mouse seemed to have disappeared. He sat up and listened carefully. There was still no sound from anyone else in the house.

"They must be heavy sleepers, that's all I can say," said Joe to himself.

Joe was scared. He wished he was anywhere but here. Someone at school had dared him to break into Kevin Bean's house and, stupidly, he had agreed to do it. Now he wished he hadn't. He knew it was wrong, and he was afraid of being caught. Joe felt around for his torch. He had to get out before anyone found him.

Joe could hear the puppy snuffling in front of him. His hand touched something hard. It felt like the torch. He was about to pick it up when the puppy grabbed the end in his mouth. After a quick tussle, Joe managed to get hold of the torch again.

Joe groaned. He couldn't believe what was happening. Then he felt a movement near his neck, and the mouse that had run up his trouser leg popped up out of the collar of his shirt. It sat there, tickling Joe's chin with its whiskers.

Joe gave a yell. "Pesky thing!" he cried. "Get off me...get off..."

Another

voice chimed in. A shrill, high voice.

"Pesky thing!" shrieked the voice, "Pesky thing," and started to cackle.

Startled, Joe turned quickly in the narrow space and tripped over a small table. He dropped the torch and fell sideways against the wall. As his fingers touched a door knob, Joe pulled it. A door opened, and he fell inside.

Inside it was very, very dark. Joe put his hands out and felt strange shapes all around him. They felt like mops and brushes and brooms. He felt them again. They *were* mops and brushes and brooms. Joe was in the broom cupboard under the stairs.

From outside he could still hear the shrill voice. "Pesky thing!" it said. "Pesky thing! Get off me, pesky thing!"

It sounded like a parrot. "Shut up," Joe called out, "you'll wake everyone."

"Shut up," repeated the parrot. "Shut up."

But it was too late. By now the whole family was awake. Joe could hear people talking. Soon they would discover him and call the police. Frightened, Joe closed the door and waited.

"Kevin, is that you making all that noise?" called Dad crossly, coming out onto the landing.

"It doesn't sound like Kevin," said Mum. Mum always stuck up for Kevin.

"Of course it's Kevin," said Grandma, coming out of her bedroom. "Who else would it be?"

"It can't be Kevin, he's been with me," said Kevin's older sister, Susie.

Now the whole family was up. They stood in a huddle on the landing and looked at each other. "It's a burglar, I bet," said Kevin, who was six and wide awake.

"Rubbish!" said Grandma. "Who'd

want to burgle us? We haven't got anything worth burgling."

"I've got a new football," said Kevin.

"He would have to be a pretty stupid burglar to break into a house just to steal a football," said Dad.

"Shall I go and look?" Kevin asked, bravely.

"You're not going on your own," said Mum.

"We'll go down together," said Grandma. "If there's anyone there, we'll soon frighten them off."

From inside the broom cupboard, Joe could hear every word. He agreed with Kevin's dad that he must be pretty stupid.

"If I keep really quiet," Joe thought to himself, "they'll give up looking and go back to bed. Then I can sneak out and no one will know."

But by now the Bean family was wide

awake. They searched the house from top to bottom looking for the intruder. They switched on all the lights. They looked in the downstairs rooms and they looked in the upstairs rooms. They looked under tables and under beds. They looked in cupboards and wardrobes. Kevin even checked inside the fridge, until he saw Grandma giving him a funny look.

But they forgot to look in the broom cupboard under the stairs.

After they had made sure that there was no one else in the house, the Bean family piled into the kitchen.

"It must have been the parrot after all," said Susie.

"That parrot's an idiot," said Dad. "If I had my way..."

"If I had my way," repeated the parrot from the dining-room, cackling loudly.

Inside the broom cupboard Joe started to relax. "It's going to be all right," he thought. "They'll go to bed soon, and then I can get out of here."

He hoped he wouldn't have to wait long. It was cramped and dark under the stairs and he didn't have anything to do. Joe hated it when he had nothing to do. He groped around for something to sit on. His hands touched a sort of crate. It seemed to be full of toys. To pass the time Joe started to examine the toys, one after the other.

There were lots of Kevin's trucks and cars. There were books and packets of crayons and pens. There were toy soldiers and a railway carriage. Then he lifted out a doll. "She must belong to Kevin's sister," said Joe, sitting the doll on his lap. As he did, the doll spoke.

"Want to go potty," she said in a clear voice.

Joe froze to the spot.

"Want to go potty," repeated the doll.

In the kitchen Grandma was tucking into tea and toast. If she woke in the night, which was often, she always had tea and toast.

"Did you hear that?" she said, a piece of toast in one hand and a cup of tea in the other.

"Hear what?" Dad asked.

Everyone stopped what they were doing and listened.

"Want to go potty," said the doll's voice again.

"It's Tiny Tots, my old doll!" said Susie. "Someone's playing with her in the broom cupboard."

The Bean family piled out of the kitchen and into the hall. They could still hear Tiny Tots' voice coming from inside the cupboard.

"Perhaps she's talking to herself," said Grandma.

"She doesn't talk unless you play with her," said Susie.

They stood still and listened. The doll was quiet. Inside the cupboard Joe was holding his breath. Kevin leaned forward and tapped on the door.

"Knock, knock! Who's there?" he asked, cheekily.

"Joe Burns," came the reply.

There was the sound of brushes and

brooms falling, and the cupboard door flew open. Still clutching the doll, Joe landed in a heap on the carpet and a little mouse, with very long whiskers, jumped off his shoulder and then disappeared into a hole in the wall.

The Bean family stared in amazement.

"Want to go potty!" cried Tiny Tots loudly. "Want to go potty!"

Joe didn't know where to look.

"Who are you?" Dad asked, angrily.

"Have you come to steal my football?" asked Kevin.

"What are you doing with Tiny Tots?"

asked Susie.

"Why are you in our broom cupboard?" yelled Grandma.

Joe looked as if he might cry.

"Leave this to me," said Mum, and she hustled everyone into the kitchen.

When the family heard that Joe had never burgled a house before and had only done it for a stupid dare, they started to feel less angry with him. Joe repeated over and over again how sorry he was.

"I don't know what came over me," he told them. "I promise I'll never do anything like it again."

"It must be exciting being a burglar," said Kevin.

"No, it's not," said Joe, shaking his head. "It's scary."

"You shouldn't have done it then," said Susie.

"I wish I hadn't," said Joe. "What I

really like doing is telling jokes and making people laugh, not burgling their houses!"

"I bet you can't make me laugh," said Grandma with a grim face.

"You never laugh at anything, do you, Gran?" said Kevin.

"Never!" said Grandma.

Joe looked at Grandma with interest.

"What has four wheels and flies?" he asked her.

"I don't know, what has four wheels and flies?" repeated Grandma.

"A van that collects rubbish!" said Joe.

Kevin giggled. Joe continued.

"What's a cow's favourite TV show?"

Gran stared at him.

"Dr Moo!" said Joe.

Kevin laughed out loud. So did Susie.

"What do you give someone who has flat feet?" Joe continued.

"I don't know," said Kevin. "What *do*

you give someone who has flat feet?"

"A foot pump!"

Mum smiled.

"Doctor, I think I'm a pair of curtains," went on Joe.

"Pull yourself together!" said Gran. She'd heard that joke before.

"What wobbles and sits in a pram?" said Joe.

"I don't know," said Dad. "What wobbles and sits in a pram?"

"A jelly baby!" said Joe. Dad smirked, then tried to hide it.

"Why can't two elephants go swimming?" Joe went on, looking straight at Grandma. She shook her head.

"Because they only have one pair of trunks!"

Kevin loved that one, and Grandma almost smiled.

"What do you call a man with no

pants?" Joe asked.

Grandma shook her head.

"Nicholas!" shouted Joe.

This was too much for Grandma. She put her hand to her mouth and started to laugh. Soon the whole family was rolling around holding their sides. Joe felt really happy. Making people laugh was such a great feeling.

Joe never broke into anyone's house again. Now he spends his spare time learning new jokes and practising being a comedian. And the other day Kevin went to a friend's party. There was a big tent in the garden, and a barbecue, and lots of games. After they'd finished playing, an older boy stood up and told some jokes. It was Joe. Some of the jokes Kevin hadn't heard before, but when Joe asked, "Why can't two elephants go swimming?" Kevin knew the answer straight away!

Do you?

To the Rescue

Rob and Rachel lived on Hideaway
Island with their parrot, Peeko.
Their house was an old caravan
that they had decorated and made into
their home. Rob and Rachel were twins.
They were the same height, had the same
colour hair and often wore the same
clothes. Everyone liked the twins. They
were always very friendly and were good at
helping out if anybody was in trouble.

Today was a very special day. They
were taking their first trip in Billy.

When they'd first arrived on the island,
they'd found a broken-down old car at the
bottom of their field. It had looked sad and
uncared for. The twins had spent weeks in

the garage fixing it up. Now the car had a brand-new engine, bright shiny windows and big sparkling headlamps that would light up the darkest night. The twins had named their car 'Billy'.

"What shall we do to celebrate our first trip in Billy?" asked Rachel.

"Picnic! Picnic!" squawked Peeko, who was perched on Billy's bonnet.

"Good idea!" said Rob, who always enjoyed a picnic.

Rachel looked up at the clear, blue sky. "It looks nice now," she said. "But the weather report says it's going to be really stormy later on."

"If it starts to rain, we'll just put Billy's roof up and come straight back," said Rob.

"Straight back! Straight back!" screeched Peeko.

"Oh, all right," laughed Rachel. "Let's get everything together, then."

It wasn't too long before they had packed their picnic basket with lots of delicious things to eat and drink.

"Everybody ready?" asked Rob, jumping into Billy.

"Ready," replied Rachel.

"Ready! Ready!" repeated Peeko.

Rob started the engine and drove down the track that led to the road.

Suddenly, he stopped. "I'm sure we've forgotten something."

"I don't think so," replied Rachel, looking through the picnic basket.

"Peeko's food! Peeko's food!" screeched Peeko.

"Of course! We've forgotten Peeko's seed," said Rob.

"Peeko get! Peeko get!" squawked Peeko, and he flew back to the caravan.

Moments later he returned, with a packet of birdseed in his beak.

"Well done, Peeko," said Rachel. "What a clever bird you are!"

"Clever Peeko! Clever Peeko!" said Peeko cheekily.

"Away we go!" said Rob, starting the engine. They drove through Whispering Wood, where the tiny fairies were supposed to live, and passed Sharks' Cove, where pirates used to bury their treasure. They drove higher and higher up the winding coast road, until they reached their favourite spot on the whole island. Chalky Rock was a clifftop, high above the beach. They could see for miles from here, and had a great view of the lighthouse.

"Well done, Billy," said Rob, proudly patting Billy's bonnet. "You drove really well."

Rachel spread a big woolly blanket on the grass. They sat down and began to unpack the picnic basket.

There were piles of peanut butter and banana sandwiches, cold drinks, fruit, biscuits and a huge chocolate cake. And, as a special treat, Rachel had brought along some homemade strawberry ice cream.

"Yummy!" said Rob, licking his lips. "It's a good thing the ice cream didn't melt on the way."

Peeko happily picked at his birdseed on the grass nearby.

The twins were feeling tired after eating so much food. They lay on their backs gazing up at the bright-blue sky.

"Aren't we lucky living on this beautiful island?" Rob asked.

"The luckiest people in the world," Rachel replied. "I wouldn't want to live anywhere else."

"Nor me! Nor me!" squawked Peeko, shrilly.

Soon, they were all fast asleep.

When they woke it was almost dark, and black clouds were rolling in from the sea.

"Looks like that storm's on its way," said Rob, peering at a ship that seemed far too close to the rocks.

"That ship's getting very near," said Rachel, anxiously.

Rob suddenly noticed that the light in the lighthouse wasn't working. This was very strange. The lighthouse was always on when it got dark.

"Look, the lighthouse isn't working," said Rob. "How will the ship know where the rocks are?"

"We'd better go and see if we can help," said Rachel.

They quickly packed away the rest of the food, and put up Billy's roof in case it started to rain. Rob started the engine and drove off towards the lighthouse. Peeko flew behind them.

By now, the wind was getting much stronger and it had begun to rain very hard.

Rob raced towards the lighthouse.

"Be careful on these wet roads," warned Rachel. "We don't want to have an accident!"

"Don't worry," replied Rob. "I won't drive too fast."

All of a sudden, a man ran out into the

middle of the road.

"Stop!" yelled the man, waving his hands.

Rob braked hard and Billy screeched to a halt. It was Fred, the lighthouse keeper.

"Are you all right, Fred?" asked Rachel.

"I'm all right," said Fred, "But the light isn't working in the lighthouse. That ship

out there is bringing in the new bulbs for it. But with no light to guide it, the ship could easily crash onto the rocks!"

"How terrible!" cried Rachel.

"Are you sure there are no more bulbs in the lighthouse?" asked Rob.

"I don't think so," replied Fred. "I've looked everywhere."

"We'll help you look, just in case. Three pairs of eyes are better than one," said Rachel.

They all piled into Billy, and Rob drove as quickly as he could along the wet road.

"Right," said Rachel, when they arrived at the lighthouse. "I think Fred and Rob should look at the top of the lighthouse, and Peeko and I will search the bottom. And we'll all meet in the middle."

"Okay!" said Rob, running up the steps. He could hear Fred hurrying up behind him. The top of the lighthouse was where the big light shone to warn ships about the dangerous rocks below. But with the light not working, the room was dark and silent.

"Have you got a torch, Fred?" asked Rob.

Fred passed him a torch and Rob searched every corner of the room for a new bulb. Looking out of the window, he saw that the ship was rocking from side to side in the heavy waves. It was getting closer and closer to the rocks.

Rachel and Peeko were searching downstairs in the rooms where Fred lived.

"Did you find anything?" she called up to Rob after a while.

"There's no bulb up here," Rob shouted.

"Nothing down here either. Let's meet in the middle room and take a look there," yelled Rachel.

The middle room was Fred's bedroom. They looked in Fred's wardrobe and behind his bookshelf. But they couldn't find a new bulb anywhere.

Suddenly, Rob saw something glinting under Fred's bed. He got down on his knees and shone the torch on it.

"I think it's a new bulb!" he cried excitedly, pulling it out.

"Well, blow me down," said Fred as Rob handed him the bulb. "You clever people. This bulb should work fine!"

"I think Peeko had better fly out to the ship and tell them that the light will soon be working again," said Rachel.

"Good idea!" said Rob. "They must be really worried by now. Be very careful, Peeko."

While Rob, Rachel and Fred climbed to the top of the lighthouse to put in the new bulb, Peeko flew out over the cliffs towards the helpless ship. The ship wasn't far away. But out at sea, the wind was so strong it kept pushing Peeko away from it.

By using all of his strength, Peeko finally landed with a loud 'squawk' on the ship's deck.

The sailors couldn't believe their eyes. What was a parrot doing on board their ship in the middle of a storm?

"Better get the captain," one of them said.

When the captain came on deck, he looked closely at Peeko, who stared right back at him.

"Light working! Light working!" Peeko suddenly squawked.

"I think he's trying to tell us that the lighthouse will soon be working," said the captain, excitedly.

"Hooray!" cheered the crew, hoping that Peeko's words would come true.

Peeko screeched loudly, then flapped his wings and flew off the ship just as quickly as he had arrived.

Meanwhile, back at the lighthouse, Rob, Rachel and Fred were just about to put the new bulb in.

"Won't be long now," said Fred, as Rob handed the precious bulb to him. Suddenly, Fred slipped. The bulb went crashing to the floor and broke into tiny pieces.

"Oh, no! What are we going to do now?" said Fred, looking down at the broken bits of glass.

"Don't worry. We'll think of something," said Rob, looking out of the window. The ship was getting nearer and nearer to the rocks.

"Those poor sailors!" cried Rachel.

Just then, Peeko flew in.

"Oh, Peeko," said Rachel. "We've broken the bulb, and don't know what else to do."

"Billy! Billy!" shrieked Peeko.

"Oh, be quiet Peeko," said Rob. "We're trying to think of what to do next."

"Billy! Billy!" shrieked Peeko again, even louder this time.

"Peeko!" warned Rob.

"Wait a minute. I think Peeko's trying to tell us something!" said Rachel.

"Billy lights! Billy lights!" squawked the parrot.

"Of course!" said Rachel. "Peeko's trying to tell us that we could use Billy's headlights to guide in the ship."

"What a brilliant idea!" cried Rob. "I'm sorry for being angry with you, Peeko," he continued, stroking Peeko's beak. "I'll go and drive Billy to the edge of the cliff and turn his lights on."

Rob ran down the steps as fast as he could, and leaped into Billy.

But when he turned the key, Billy wouldn't start.

"Oh, no!" he thought. "What else can go wrong?"

He tried and tried, but Billy just wouldn't go.

"Quick! Billy won't start! We'll have to push him!" he yelled up to the others.

Rachel and Fred ran down and they all began to push Billy. After one push, luckily he started.

Rob quickly turned Billy around and drove him to the very edge of the cliff. As

soon as they were there, he positioned Billy
so that his lights shone out to sea.

"I hope we're not too late," said Rob
anxiously.

They stared in silence, hoping their
plan would work.

The wind howled around them and the
rain had already soaked them wet through.

They could see the ship being tossed around in the storm like a matchstick. By now, it was only moments away from crashing into the rocks.

"It's never going to make it. It's far too close!" cried Rachel.

Then suddenly, at the last possible moment, the ship seemed to turn away from the rocks.

"It's seen Billy's lights!" yelled Rachel.

"Oh, I hope so," cried Fred.

"Come on! Come on!" shouted Rob.

"Come on! Come on!" squawked Peeko.

Gradually the ship turned, narrowly missing the jagged rocks.

"It's done it! It's done it!" Rob cried.

"Thank goodness for that," said Rachel.

"That was a close one," Fred sighed.

"Close one! Close one!" copied Peeko.

Rob kept Billy's lights on until the ship had reached the island's harbour.

As soon as the ship had docked, the twins and Fred rushed down to greet the captain and his crew.

"I can't thank you enough!" cried the captain, walking towards them. "You saved our lives!"

"It's Peeko you need to thank," said Rachel, smiling proudly.

"Clever Peeko! Clever Peeko!" screeched Peeko happily.

"Come to the lighthouse and have some hot soup to warm you up," said Fred. "Oh, and bring the lightbulbs with you!"

"We've got some sandwiches left that need eating too," said Rob, grabbing the picnic basket.

They all sat down in the brightly lit, warm lighthouse and tucked into the food.

"What an adventure! Hooray for

Peeko!" cried the sailors.

"Hooray for Peeko! Hooray for Peeko!" squawked Peeko.

And they all agreed that Peeko was a very clever parrot indeed!